The Wizard of Oz

Illustrated by Mauro Evangelista

Retold by Rosie Dickins

Based on the story by L. Frank Baum

Dorothy lived on a lonely farm in Kansas,
with her Uncle Henry and Aunt Em
and her little dog, Toto.

woof!

One day, the wind began to howl.
"It's a whirlwind!" cried Aunt Em.
"Everyone to the cellar!"

But Toto had dashed for
cover under the bed.

The wind blew harder...

and harder...

until suddenly...

it spun the house into the air.

The house sailed through the sky...
and landed with a **BUMP!**

Dorothy poked her head outside
and saw some friendly faces.

"Welcome to Oz!"

"Please, how do I get home?" she asked.

"You'll need to see the wizard," said
a woman. "He lives in Emerald City,
at the end of the yellow brick road."

And she gave Dorothy a pair of
sparkling silver shoes for the journey.

Dorothy's new shoes tinkled on the yellow bricks, as she walked along the road.

"Hello there!" called a scarecrow.
"Where are you going?"

"To see the wizard," replied Dorothy.

"Can I come?" said the scarecrow. "I want
to ask the wizard for some brains."

"Of course," said Dorothy,
with a smile.

A few miles on, they saw a tinman. He stood stock still, his arms stuck behind his head. "Help!" he grunted. "I've rusted up."

Dorothy picked up a nearby oilcan and trickled oil onto his stiff joints. "We're on our way to see the wizard," she said.

"Can I come?" asked the tinman. "I want to ask the wizard for a heart."

They had barely set off again, when a lion leaped out of the trees with a terrible **ROAR!** The scarecrow trembled but Toto barked.

"Oh!" yelped the lion. "Don't hurt me."

"I heard you talking about the wizard and I want him to make me brave.
Let me come with you."

The four of them followed the yellow
brick road as it wound on and on,
past forests and rivers and fields.

At last, they came to a city of glittering emeralds.

A gatekeeper gave them each a pair of green glasses and led them to the wizard's palace.

"I'll help you, if you help me," said the wizard.

"First, you must kill the wicked witch!"

The wicked witch lived in a castle guarded by wolves and crows.

Gnnnnn

But the tinman fought
off the wolves.

And the scarecrow scared away the crows.

Furious, the witch summoned her flying monkeys.
Soon the friends were prisoners in her castle.

"Now you're my slaves," she cackled.

"Get to work!"

Then the witch noticed Dorothy's beautiful silver shoes.

"I want those shoes," thought the witch.

She waited until
Dorothy was fetching
a pail of water...

...then she
pushed her
and pounced.

Dorothy was so annoyed, she threw the water all over the witch.

At once, the witch melted away into a puddle.

"She's gone!" cried Dorothy, quickly putting on her shoes. "We can claim our rewards."

The wizard's rewards were rather strange.

First, he gave
the scarecrow a
handful of pins.

"Now I'm as sharp as a pin."

Then he gave
the tinman a
heart-shaped
cushion.

And for the lion, there was
a bottle marked Courage.

Last of all, the wizard showed
Dorothy a hot-air balloon.
"We'll fly home!" he said.

But the ropes snapped and the balloon took off without her.
"Go to the good witch Glinda!" called the wizard. "She'll help you."

Dorothy was in despair, but her friends took her to Glinda's palace.

"I'm stuck in Oz!" Dorothy sobbed,

standing before the throne.

"Don't worry," said Glinda, kindly.
"The silver shoes will take you home."
"Just knock the heels together and wish."

Dorothy and Toto whirled through the air... and landed back on the farm. There stood Aunt Em, in front of a brand-new farmhouse.

Dorothy ran up and threw her arms around her. "I've been on an amazing adventure," she said. "But oh! I'm so glad to be home."

And Toto barked as if to say, "Me too!"

Designed by Louise Flutter, Laura Wood and Emily Bornoff
Digital design: John Russell
Edited by Jenny Tyler and Lesley Sims